Praise for *9 Holes of Fear*

"Johnny, your book finally puts to words what so many young people and beginners feel about the game of golf. Jordan, I am delighted that you have enjoyed playing the Bayonet at Ft. Ord. Taking on a challenge like the Bayonet course illustrates that it is possible to turn the fears of golf into joy! As a golf course architect, I will keep in mind what I have learned from this wonderful book and continue designing golf courses that are fun for everyone."

—Gene Bates, Golf Course Architect
Designed Fred Couples and Johnny Miller Courses

"This book is a wonderfully illustrated story that is fun to read with the bonus of a great message that people of all ages will be able to relate to."

—Rudy Duran, PGA Member, Tiger Woods' First Golf Coach

"The game of golf, like the game of life, is full of ups and downs as well as twists and turns. Solving its problems is the true essence for which the rewards are greater than could be imagined."

—Eddie Merrins, The Little Pro

"When you are young it's hard to understand the importance of a good mental game. But this book is the perfect tool to give every kid, golfer or not, in order to teach him or her how to dig deep inside and get through anything that comes their way."

—Marcia Wallis, Stanford Women's Golf Team, 1999-2003

"What a great read for youngsters and their parents to discuss basic life principles of individual responsibility, self esteem and compassion for others. Lil' Jordan's maturation into young adolescence is replete with these traits. Kids will remember the advice in the story as they move from the playground to the boardroom."

—Bruce T. Cooper, Esq., CEO, Electronic Courthouse

"For a gifted young golfer like Lil' Jordan to be exposed to the limelight all the time, it is hard to imagine that he wouldn't be a bit full of himself. He is exactly the opposite. I have never met a more humble, down to earth "kid." The life-lessons of golf are firmly established in this young man's life. No wonder, he had the perfect teacher in his dad, Johnny. Johnny's book is a treat and full of excellent examples of how to prepare any youngster for the course of life."

—John Aylward, Actor (*ER, West Wing*)

"I loved the book. Even though the book is intended for children, I believe that adults will also find it to be an enjoyable read. Adults can certainly relate to each of those "monsters." It was very creative how you turned the troubles into "monsters." A very good book for a parent and child to read together."

—Rusty Stockton, Executive Director, Salinas Valley Jr. Golf Association

ISBN-13: 978-1-60747-703-7
Library of Congress Cataloging-In-Publication Data Available

Layout Design by Sonia Fiore
Illustration by Ryan Benjamin

Printed in the United States of America

Dove Books, Inc.
9465 Wilshire Boulevard, Suite 840
Beverly Hills, CA 90212

10 9 8 7 6 5 4 3 2 1

LIL' JORDAN'S
'9 HOLES OF FEAR

CREATED AND WRITTEN BY
JOHNNY EUGENIO

ILLUSTRATED BY
RYAN BENJAMIN

DOVE
BOOKS

One sunny afternoon, Jordan and his dad were watching their favorite golfer play on television. Jordan was amazed to see such great golf shots and the players having so much fun.

"Daddy, can you teach me how to play golf?" Jordan asked.

His dad replied, "Jordan, I would love to teach you, but I know a great golf teacher who could really help you learn the game better."

"One day I am going to play golf in a tournament and win a trophy just like those golfers do on television!" Jordan exclaimed.

So Jordan began to take lessons with the golf professional. After school, Jordan's dad would pick him up and take him to his lessons. He worked hard and learned quickly, and he had a lot of fun.

One day his dad decided it was time to go to the New Golf Course to play a few holes together. Jordan was excited to show his dad what he had learned.

As they approached the putting green they were met by Lee, the club president of the New Golf Course.

Lee pointed to a sign that read, "NO KIDS ALLOWED."

Jordan and his dad were confused and asked why children weren't allowed to play on the New Golf Course.

Lee said, "There are many reasons why kids shouldn't play. Golf isn't for kids—they should wait until they are at least teenagers to play. Some courses have alligators, mountain lions, rattlesnakes, bears, foxes, coyotes, and even a BOGEY MONSTER."

Jordan asked, "Did you say Bogey Monster?"

Lee said, "Of course. He could be hiding anywhere on the putting green."

Jordan and his dad laughed. Then Jordan's dad said he would try to find another golf course that let kids play, and they said goodbye to Lee.

As they were walking away, Jordan's dad said, "There are many golf courses where children aren't allowed to play, but one day you will be able to play on all of them."

Later that day, Jordan was on the driving range hitting golf balls when his neighbor, Bill, approached him.

"Jordan, I am so glad you're hitting golf balls on the driving range instead of hitting my house with them," said Bill.

Jordan looked alarmed and replied, "Sir, I'm sorry about hitting your house. I didn't know I could hit that far, so now I practice here."

Bill smiled and mentioned to Jordan that he just joined the New Golf Course. Then Bill added, "I know your dad doesn't agree, but I think Lee is right. Kids shouldn't be allowed to play the course."

Jordan didn't say anything to Bill, but he felt sad that he would never get a chance to play on the New Golf Course.

Just then a lady by the name of Marcia walked up to them. She introduced herself and was surprised to hear that the New Golf Course would not allow kids. She told Jordan and Bill that she played when she was young like Jordan and eventually played for the Stanford University college golf team.

Marcia said, "Bill, I believe that all children who are as mature and disciplined as Jordan should be allowed to play golf."

Bill thought for a minute, then said, "Well, maybe I can take Jordan to the New Golf Course on Mondays when the course is closed. I'll ask Lee. It's worth a try."

"And Jordan, I'll take you to play on the Stanford golf course one day. You'll have fun playing it," Marcia said before she went back to hitting long drives with her beautiful swing.

Excited and hopeful, Jordan began practicing again in earnest. His next drive was his longest ever!

Finally the day arrived when Bill told Jordan's dad that he had talked to Lee, the club president. Lee reluctantly had given Bill permission to take Jordan to play the first nine holes at the New Golf Course.

The only condition that Lee placed on the game was that Jordan could only play with a member, and his father was not allowed to be with him. So Bill agreed to take Jordan and watch over him.

Jordan's mom carefully packed his bag with some necessities. She said to him, "You have a jacket in your bag along with some water, a candy bar, and a hat. You never know when the weather might change, and you have to be prepared in case it does."

Like any mom would do, she reminded Jordan to stay away from mountain cliffs and water hazards, and to stay close to Bill and Lee. Jordan's mom played the sport of golf, too, so she wanted to make sure her son watched out for any possible dangers.

Jordan's dad made sure Jordan had everything he would need to play:

- new golf balls
- clubs
- golf tees
- a divot repair tool
- a permanent marker
- a ball marker
- gloves
- his cell phone
- sunscreen

Jordan was now all set for his big day playing golf!

Jordan's father dropped him off at the golf course, leaving him with Bill. Lee walked up and said, "Oh, I remember you. You came with your dad and tried to sneak onto our course. You're lucky you know Bill or you would never have a chance to play here," he said sternly.

"Thank you, sir, for inviting me to play. I can't wait to play the first nine holes on the New Course," Jordan said, polite as could be. Then Jordan added, "If I behave and play well, can all my friends come out to play this course too?"

Lee laughed and replied, "Kid, if you can handle the '9 Holes of Fear' and defeat the Bogey Monster, then every kid in the world can play here."

Jordan smiled and eagerly accepted the challenge.

Bill added, "And I'll even build a special clubhouse for all of your friends if you can beat all '9 Holes of Fear.' And in that clubhouse, there will be a game room with a pool table, video games, and even your own golf simulator station."

Jordan couldn't believe what he was hearing and called his dad to tell him all about it. Jordan's dad was so excited that he told everyone in town about the deal.

But Jordan had no idea what was to going to happen next.

Minutes later, Jordan stood on the first tee and prepared to hit the ball.

All of a sudden, a tornado-like wind began to blow, and Jordan was frightened.

Then a scary brown creature with spikes on his back appeared.

The creature said, "I am the Bogey Monster. When I am done with you, you will never want to play golf again."

Bill and Lee looked at Jordan and wondered whether Jordan could actually win the "9 Holes of Fear."

Jordan quickly learned that the 1st hole of fear was where the Pressure Monster likes to hide. This monster pops out and gets under the golfer's skin, making him nervous as he steps on the first tee box.

Jordan remembered what his golf coach said during practice not too long ago: "Get behind the ball and make sure you are aligned with the target. Also, make sure you have a good grip, a good stance, and think about the target you are going to hit."

Just as Jordan was about to swing, Bill and Lee started talking loudly. Then their cell phones began ringing, cars passing by started honking, a train rumbled by, and an airplane flew over.

As if all that was not enough to distract him, the two men demanded, "Hurry up and hit the ball, Jordan. We don't have all day."

The Pressure Monster was doing a good job, but Jordan focused like his coach had instructed and smacked the ball right down the fairway.

The Pressure Monster looked confused and slunk back into his hole. Bill and Lee couldn't believe Jordan hit the ball straight and won the 1st hole!

On the 2nd hole, Jordan faced the Tree Monster.

Lee mentioned that this monster was known to grab your golf ball in mid-flight. "He will sometimes even steal your ball and hide it on the other side of the course. He is known for blocking your shot and laughing at you," Lee said.

Jordan remembered what his coach said about using the right club to hit over branches that are too high, or to keep it low when trying to place the ball under a tree.

The talented little golfer stepped up and hit his ball over the tree, and then chipped it under. And just like that, the Tree Monster was defeated. The monster curled up like a tree trunk and disappeared with a frown.

Jordan smiled and began walking to the next hole.

Bill and Lee had surprised looks on their faces, but they both knew there were still seven monsters left for Jordan to beat in order to win the challenge.

The 3rd hole was home to the Grass Monster.

Jordan was told that the Grass Monster is tall and thick, and he sucks your ball beneath the soil and hides it.

Bill warned Jordan, "The monster also grabs onto your ball when you hit it. Sometimes it takes more than one swing to get out of his grasp."

But Jordan's coach appeared in his head. He remembered from his golf lesson to take a lofted club and swing through the ball.

And with that in mind, Jordan swung and knocked the ball out with ease!

The Grass Monster was left with nothing but a good haircut!

That left six more monsters for Jordan to meet and defeat.

As Jordan continued to play the course, Bill and Lee tried to scare him, telling him that the 4th hole is home to the fierce and undefeatable Water Monster.

When they got to the water hazard, the little golfer looked calm and in control. But then a huge screen of mist appeared, and when it cleared the Water Monster stood tall like a huge wave with his watery mouth wide open.

The Water Monster was eagerly waiting for little Jordan!

A golfer nearby warned Jordan, "Hitting the ball into the Water Monster's home sucks the life right out of some golfers, and they will talk about it for years!"

Lee added, "And golfers have been known to quit the game just because they hit too many balls into the water."

And Bill chimed in, "And some will never visit a course with water again!"

Jordan's coach appeared again in his mind.

Coach reminded Jordan to make sure he had the right club and to check that he was the right distance away from the ball. Jordan looked through his bag for the correct club, then carefully adjusted his distance from the ball.

When Jordan felt he was all set, he swung and smacked the ball all the way over the water hazard, onto the other side of the green.

"Hooray!" Jordan shouted. "The Water Monster has been defeated!"

Bill and Lee were shocked by the results of Jordan's game thus far. They shook their heads in amazement.

But Jordan just kept playing well. And believe it or not, he didn't seem the least bit concerned about the monsters he had been encountering.

The 5th hole, which was where Jordan walked next, was where the Weather Monster lived.

Lee, wagging his finger, warned Jordan, "He will make golfers stop playing, and they end up going home because it's just too hot or too cold. Most golfers are not prepared when this monster comes out. They forget to bring an umbrella or warm clothing. The Weather Monster can also make golf scores increase, which also discourages some golfers from playing."

Jordan was wondering what this monster was going to do to him today, when all of a sudden, he became thirsty, and then cold, and then hungry, and felt like going home. This was definitely the Weather Monster at work!

But the young golfer remembered that his mom had packed his jacket and some food, so he reached into his bag and put on his coat and hat. Then he ate his candy bar and drank his water. Now Jordan felt better and was ready to face the monster!

The monster could not believe Jordan was so prepared and knew he didn't have a chance of defeating Jordan now...so he vanished!

Bill and Lee were becoming worried—things were definitely not going as planned.

Up next was the 6th hole. Bill warned Jordan that this was the home of the Green Monster. "He is often called 'The Snake' or 'The Three Putt King,'" Bill said.

Lee explained, "His job is to confuse you by making your ball go the wrong way or by slowing it down after you hit it. Most golfers lose all their strokes on the green. This monster can quickly convince you to quit and could also make you never want to play the game again."

Just then, the Green Monster came up out of the ground with a crown on his head and looked at Jordan, hoping to scare him off the course.

Jordan's coach appeared again in his mind. He remembered his recent lesson about putting, so he reached into his bag and took out his putter. Jordan squatted behind the ball to take a look at which direction it would roll. He took a practice putt and then hit it right into the hole!

The monster became so angry that he began shaking like an earthquake, and his crown fell off.

Jordan was amazed that he conquered the Green Monster and quickly ran to the 7th hole.

Bill and Lee were already at the 7th hole talking to the Sand Monster when Jordan arrived. When Bill and Lee spotted Jordan, they came over to him and pulled him into a huddle.

"This monster is one of the most feared," Lee whispered to Jordan. "He loves to make you think you can hit it out of the bunker on the first try. Most golfers who are trapped in the sand may take many strokes to get out."

Bill added, "The Sand Monster sometimes makes you stand funny while trying to hit the ball. Then he laughs at you when the ball lands in the dirt, looking like a fried egg."

This time Jordan's coach appeared again in his thoughts but the image was so vivid, it was almost like he was there right next to him. Coach said, "Jordan, remember not to set your club on the sand before you hit the ball. Hit behind the ball and make sure you grab the sand. Don't stop your swing."

So Jordan took his coach's advice and hit an amazing shot! He was out of the sand on his very first try.

The Sand Monster was waving his arms like a basketball player trying to block a shot. He sank back into his hole and was defeated too, just like all the monsters before him.

The course was very quiet as Jordan approached the 8th hole.

Bill and Lee told Jordan they would go on ahead and meet him on the 9th hole because the last monster was the scariest. They thought for sure it would be the monster that would defeat Jordan.

Bill warned Jordan as they headed off, "The monster who lives over here is called the O.B. Monster. He is also known as the ghost who sends your ball out of bounds as soon as you take a swing. This monster always hangs out by the landing areas of the hole and lines himself up along the fairway like tombstones laid out in a cemetery. If this monster gets you, your score and your feelings will be hurt, your golfing buddies will feel sorry for you, and you may always hold onto that disappointing memory."

As soon as Bill and Lee were out of sight, the O.B. Monster appeared and looked at Jordan with his one eye, showing off his big teeth. But Jordan ignored him and lined up to the ball. Jordan's coach appeared in his head again and

reminded him to block out all fear and think positively. Jordan thanked his coach in his mind and hit a great shot right down the fairway.

The ball bounced near the white O.B. markers but was safe! Jordan could not have defeated any of the monsters without the lessons he received from his coach.

Jordan called his dad and let him know that he defeated all the monsters but one. Then Jordan's dad called everyone and told them to meet his son on the 9th hole, because history was about to be made. That is, children might be allowed to play the New Course, and a new clubhouse might be built!

Then all of a sudden, the Bogey Monster appeared and approached Jordan on his way to the 9th hole. He snarled as he said, "You may have defeated the first eight monsters, but you'll never defeat me!" Jordan hurried on his way, looking over his shoulder as the monster followed along the course.

Bill and Lee gleefully told Jordan about the rules for the last hole. Jordan would have to defeat the club champion! They were sure there was no way Jordan would ever beat him!

Jordan waited patiently as he saw all his friends and family show up near the 9th hole. They came running to the little golfer as he stood on the ninth tee box. His best friend Reggie saw him and gave Jordan a nod and a "thumbs up."

Suddenly, the Bogey Monster turned himself into the club champion. With all the excitement, no one noticed except Jordan. Now he knew that the club champion was really the Bogey Monster in disguise. This would be a real challenge!

Lee made an announcement to the news reporters and other people watching: "In order for Lil' Jordan to win this challenge, he has to defeat our club champion." The crowd cheered and shouted, "Jordan can do it!" and "Go, Lil' Jordan, go!"

The hole was a Par 4 and 385 yards. The crowd looked amazed as the club champion hit 245 yards down the middle.

Jordan took a deep breath and hit his ball 165 yards down the middle.

The Bogey Monster, or club champion as he appeared to everyone else, walked with Jordan down the fairway, teasing him, and asked if he had taken his vitamins today or eaten a balanced breakfast.

Jordan lost focus and hit his next shot only 80 yards. His ball was right next to the Bogey Monster's ball.

It took Jordan two shots to catch up to the Bogey Monster. The Bogey Monster hit his next shot within 10 feet of the hole.

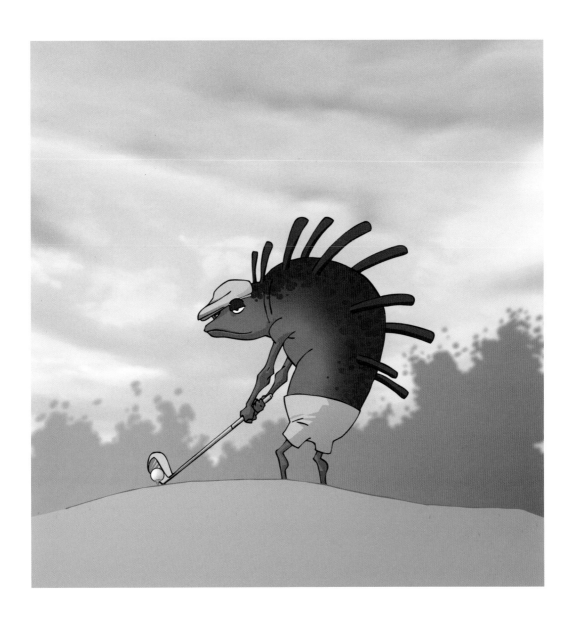

Jordan's friends slowly started to bow their heads in defeat. Jordan looked worried, too, and couldn't believe what was happening. He collected his thoughts and tried to focus on his next shot.

And just when he was about to hit it, he noticed that the ball was not his.

He turned to the Bogey Monster and said, "You hit my ball on the green. I am playing a ball with a green stripe, and you are playing a ball with two blue dots. That is a two-stroke penalty!"

Jordan's best friend Reggie yelled out, "Jordan can still win!" The crowd started cheering once again.

The Bogey Monster could not believe he hit the wrong ball. He was too busy mocking Jordan to pay attention to what he was doing.

Jordan hit his next shot onto the green using his new hybrid club. The Bogey Monster hit his fourth shot into the sand bunker. Then he hit his fifth shot on the green, and it rolled into the hole.

Lee yelled out, "If Jordan ties the club champion, they will have to play this hole again!"

Jordan looked over to the crowd and noticed his coach had come out to the course to see him win this challenge. Coach gave him a confident look to let Jordan know he was very proud of his pupil.

Jordan looked at his parents and smiled. And shortly after, he lined up the putt and made the shot with ease!

After the winning shot, all of Jordan's friends and family ran up to him. Bill and Lee made an announcement to everyone.

Lee said, "Little Jordan just showed me that a young kid can play golf and handle many challenges out on the course. I was surprised that a kid could play such great golf at such a young age. I promised Jordan that if he could defeat the '9 Holes of Fear,' I would allow kids to play this course." The crowd applauded Lee.

Then Bill added, "I really didn't think Jordan could do it, but he did. I promised to build a special clubhouse for all the children with their own game room if Jordan could win the challenge. So Lee and I will do what we promised, and kids are now welcome here at the New Golf Course!"

And just after the announcement was made, Lee removed the old sign that read, "NO KIDS ALLOWED."

Then Jordan said, "I want to thank Bill and Lee for letting me play here today. Now all kids who are my age and all of my friends can play this beautiful course. I want to thank my golf teacher and coach, Mr. Merrins, who taught me many lessons and life skills, and also my parents, for allowing me to play this great game." Jordan hugged his parents as they smiled proudly.

Jordan yelled out, "Lil' Jordan and the Clubhouse Kids!"

THE END

Jordan Eugenio

NICKNAME: Lil Jordan **MEMBER CLUB:** The First Tee of Monterey County **AGE:** 11 **WEBSITE:** www.liljordan.com **FAMILY:** Parents and seven siblings **TALENTS:** Golf and music emanate from the fast-growing Jordan Eugenio. The aspiring actor, known as the "Ambassador of Junior Golf and Hip Hop," has performed at events ranging from Michael Irvin's celebrity golf tournament in 2006 to the Ryder Cup and an impending performance at the NBA All-Star Game. **MUSICAL STYLE:** Rap music, hip hop and R&B define the Marina resident's style, but a desire to give back permeates his outlook on life. Eugenio's first song, "Swing for the Dream," was produced to educate other children about kids with disabilities. The song appears on the 11-year-old's album, "RU Ready for Me?" and is a tribute to his brother Joshua, who has down syndrome. Jordan is finalizing a deal with BDA Sports, the same sports agency that represents Yao Ming and Carmelo Anthony and will soon host "Make it Pro," an online television program geared for kids. **INSPIRATION:** "I got started because of Tiger Woods. My dad taught me when I was two, like Tiger's dad. I used to wear Tiger's Sunday red shirt all the time but now I like to wear European styles." **GAME:** "I'm more accurate now and my game got better as I got older. I'm really working on my short game." **FAVORITES:** "I like Will Smith because he is an actor

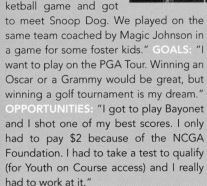

and a clean rapper. He's not into the gangsterish rap. I like Eminem, because people doubted him, but he achieved his dream. I also like the Beatles." **OTHERS:** "Inspiring other kids is really important to me. I played in a charity basketball game and got to meet Snoop Dog. We played on the same team coached by Magic Johnson in a game for some foster kids." **GOALS:** "I want to play on the PGA Tour. Winning an Oscar or a Grammy would be great, but winning a golf tournament is my dream." **OPPORTUNITIES:** "I got to play Bayonet and I shot one of my best scores. I only had to pay $2 because of the NCGA Foundation. I had to take a test to qualify (for Youth on Course access) and I really had to work at it."

This book is dedicated to my wife and my children's great mother Maria, and my 8 children: Johnny II, Joshua, Jordan, Justin, Jayson, Jayden, Eric, and Shayla. Thanks to my parents Rudy and Helen for their love and support.

My son Jordan was an inspiration to me when he started golfing at two years old. He is the reason I needed to encourage more children to play the sport of golf. I want to share my experiences, which could be shared with all the children over the world and could inspire them to keep trying harder when challenges arise. This book will allow parents and grandparents to share their positive and challenging memories about a sport they love.

My biggest inspiration has been my other son, Joshua, who has Down Syndrome. He has given me the strength to never give up. He is teaching me the real meaning of life He always reminds me to share his story and to educate people about kids with disabilities.

I hope you enjoy the first book on Lil' Jordan.

Eugenio Enterprises Inc.

About the Illustrator

Ryan Benjamin has been in the entertainment industry as an artist and designer for 14 years. He began as a comic book artist for Image Comics/ Wildstorm studios back in 1993. He worked on a variety of comics; learning from various industry professionals like Mark Silvestry, Whilce Portacio, Scott Williams and Jim Lee. Eventually he expanded and began to draw comics for other comic book studios like Dark Horse, Marvel and DC Comics. Drawing comics allowed him to explore other areas in the art industry. Video games became that second vehicle he needed to do that. Since then he has worked on a variety of video games and short films. Aspiring to learn and expand everyday, he continues to develop comics, video games and films for a variety of projects.

www.ryanbenjamin.com

GOLF IS FUN TO PLAY AND EASY TO LOVE,

GOLF TEACHES IMPORTANT LESSONS AND CHALLENGES YOU TO BE YOUR BEST.

PING thinks golf is the greatest game in the world. That's why we make golf clubs for young golfers. We want you to have fun and hope that you'll love the game as much as we do.

BRING A SMILE TO YOUR FACE AND JOY TO YOUR HEART.

PING
PLAY YOUR BEST™